W9-ASR-054

3 8749 0048 2078 0

THE GREAT CANNON BEACH MOUSE CAPER

SPIRIT of St.LOOSE

SUNDERLAND

PETER WAUGH

ILLUSTRATED BY DON SUNDERLAND

Published by:
Educare Press
2802 NW Market, Suite 308
Seattle, WA 98107

Printed and bound in Canada.
10 9 8 7 6 5 4 3 2 1

First Edition
Library of Congress Catalog Card Number: 2002100802

ISBN: O-944638-38-4

To my mother, Mary Littlejohn Waugh, who was first to tell me stories; to my English teacher Miss Wilson, Dalkeith High School (1950-1956), who first suggested I could write them; and to my wife, Margaret and our children, James and Leila for their endless patience and support.

Peter Waugh

Avec merci et amour à ma grandmère Zoe Miranda Dease.

Don Sunderland

CHAPTER ONE

THE MUSEUM MICE

In St Louis there is a museum. As museums go, it is not very impressive. But, for many years, one of the largest communities of mice in the whole city has been taking residence in its basement. Compared with other communities, in a baker's shop say, or maybe a cheese factory, life has never been easy for the museum mice. Families that choose to settle here are seeking something other than security: education. Over the years, youngsters growing up in the museum environment have earned the reputation of being the brightest and most creative mice in the city. Museum mice have respect.

The permanent displays in the museum cover a wide variety of subjects: American history, industrial history, exploration, scientific progress, and so much more. The youngsters in the community absorb the knowledge passed on by their parents and teachers. But it is in the evening when their education

Bert and other impatient youngsters slipped into the exhibition hall.

truly comes alive. When the museum closes at six PM and all the people are gone, the teacher mice escort their students through the various exhibition rooms. The dioramas of prehistoric creatures, famous battles, and the Pyramids of Egypt mesmerize and fascinate the young mice.

And then there are the special traveling exhibits that passed through the museum, exhibits about the voyages of Captain Cook or the first men on the moon. It was at one such exhibit that two of the community's youngsters, Bert and Mavis first became acquainted.

Up to that time Bert's hunger for knowledge filled his life. He devoured information like other mice devoured cheese.

When he learned that the *Lewis & Clark* exhibition was coming to the museum, Bert's excitement was greater than ever. The story of their pioneering 1803 journey from St. Louis to the Pacific coast had always thrilled him.

The rattling of the custodian's cart was still echoing through the museum when Bert and other impatient youngsters slipped into the exhibition hall. The display lights had been left on for security.

Bert's eyes drank in the array of artifacts, maps, diaries, guns, clothes and equipment. He marveled at seeing some of the original items from the actual expedition.

As the exhibition moved into its second week much of the original interest began to drop off. With each passing day, fewer and fewer mice visited the exhibits. But for Bert there was no faltering of his interest. Even during sleep, he would dream of the mist-wreathed pine forests and the roaring surf of the Pacific Northwest.

Bert wasn't the only mouse fascinated by the story of Lewis and Clark. Mavis, another bright, young mouse, continued to visit the exhibition long after the other mice lost interest. Mavis was an adventurous spirit and was intrigued by their journey, too. The vital part played by Sacagawea, the young Indian girl, in the success of the expedition had always been a source of inspiration to her. However as time passed she found her attention being diverted towards the handsome, if somewhat intense, Bert.

It took some time before this attention was returned, but returned it was. The first shy and hesitant exchange quickly blossomed into animated conversations about exploration and pioneering journeys that continued long after *Lewis & Clark* had moved on.

Bert was delighted to find someone who shared his thirst for knowledge and adventure, someone who treated his every word with wonder and respect. She was also very pretty.

Mavis, in turn, admired his infectious enthusiasm and ambition to do great things. Their friendship grew by leaps and bounds. It carried on through the remainder of their schooling and beyond.

Then one day, at a simple ceremony held in the basement of a local church, they became husband and wife.

Bert and Mavis began teaching at the community school and they set up home in a cozy drawer of a discarded desk in the basement. The first few months passed blissfully and each evening they would chatter enthusiastically about the challenges of the teaching profession.

But as the year moved into the muggy days of summer, Mavis began to notice lapses in Bert's normally upbeat spirit. He was never short-tempered, but there were times when she would find him deep in thought, a faraway look in his eyes.

One night, after dinner, she voiced her concerns.

"Is something troubling you Bert? Is it the school?"

Bert's eyebrows shot up in apparent surprise. "The school? No!" He gave a rather forced grin. "The kids are just the same little monsters they have always been."

Mavis would not be brushed off. "Don't pretend with me, Bert. I know you better than that. What's wrong?"

The smile faded from Bert's face. "School's fine Mavis. I really enjoy teaching, but ... "

"But what, Bert?"

He did not answer right away.

Mavis swallowed hard. "Is it ... us?"

Bert quickly leaned over and kissed her cheek. "Of course, not Mavis. You're the best thing that has ever happened to me."

Mavis smiled with relief, but still she was not satisfied. "Well, what is it then, Bert?"

He shrugged. "I suppose I think I may be in a rut ... a comfortable rut."

"Maybe we need to get away for awhile. Do you want to travel? Is that it?"

"I did have a dream last night. About Lewis and Clark. I was with them when they reached the Pacific"

Bert shrugged his shoulders. "I did have a dream last night. About Lewis and Clark. I was with them when they reached the Pacific. It seemed so real."

Mavis fell silent for a few moments. "Why don't we do the same?"

Bert's eyes opened wide in surprise, "Do you mean that, Mavis?"

She gave him a playful shove. "Of course I mean it. But we better make it soon."

Bert was baffled. "What do you mean?"

Mavis broke into a fit of laughter. Bert looked even more bewildered. Mavis made an effort to bring her amusement under control. "Because it will be easier to travel if there are only the two of us?"

"You mean you are ... we are?" Bert stumbled over the words.

Mavis giggled once more. "I just found out today. You're going to be a daddy, Bert."

The first few months passed blissfully.

CHAPTER TWO

UNCLE THOMAS

Bert's Uncle Thomas ran the most prestigious travel agency in the city, Mouse Trips International. From his office in the basement cellar of a large trucking company warehouse, Uncle Thomas enjoyed an unblemished reputation for service excellence. He took great pride in upholding the company motto: *Don't despair, we'll get you there.*

The operational process was deceptively simple. The warehouse was a central depot for a trucking company, from which goods were shipped to all parts of the country and beyond. A mouse wishing transport to Washington, DC might travel in a crate of automobile air filters. A California-bound traveler could be transported in a box of computer parts. St. Louis mice just had to state a desired destination and Uncle Thomas would arrange it.

Bert and Mavis wasted no time. The evening following their decision to go west, they showed up at Uncle Thomas's office. The waiting room was teeming with mice of all ages, shapes, and sizes.

Confusion reigned as some of the less experienced travelers criss-crossed the room. Others sat with their backs against the wall with the bored look of veteran travelers.

One of Uncle Thomas's assistants escorted them to a waiting area, informing them that he would be free to meet with them shortly.

At first Bert and Mavis felt intimidated by the intensity of the place and sat quietly in one corner. But the sense of adventure that hung in the air was infectious and soon they were watching the antics of their fellow travelers with great interest. An MTI employee appeared at a doorway.

"MTI Trip Number 37, New York via Pittsburgh and Philadelphia will be boarding in fifteen minutes. All ticket holding passengers please exit through departure hole Number Six," she called out. A murmur rose from the waiting crowds and a dozen or so mice scurried out of sight through Number Six.

Almost immediately another employee appeared.

"MTI international flight Number 109, London via Boston is now boarding through Hole Number Two," he announced. A small number of rather self-satisfied looking mice headed for Hole Number Two. They moved with the slow and dignified gait of V.I.M.s. Very Important Mice. They pretended to be oblivious to the awed looks cast in their direction by their less sophisticated fellow travelers.

Mavis was impressed. "London, Bert? Just imagine. London!"

He did not have time to reply. An assistant arrived to escort them through a hole, above which was a sign reading, "EMPLOYEES ONLY BEYOND THIS POINT."

They were ushered into a surprisingly plain little room. "Mr. Thomas will be with you shortly," she said, disappearing out the door. A large map of the United States covered one wall and on the opposite wall was a map of the world. The unmistakable odor of cheese filled the room. Suddenly, a door in the wall facing them swung open and in bustled Uncle Thomas, accompanied by an even stronger smell of cheese.

Uncle Thomas had emigrated from England many years previous but the accent that greeted them was undiluted by the passage of time.

"How delightful to see you, Albert. And always a pleasure to see you, Mavis, my dear." He twirled his whiskers. "Now what can I do for you both?" He beamed a toothy smile. "Spot of vacation maybe?

He pointed to the map. "Look where it is!

Jolly good idea." He scurried over to the map of the United States. "Ah hah! The very thing. Sunshine special ... Florida. Half price." He gave an apologetic smile. "Crate of bad oranges being sent back to Orlando. Might pong a bit of course, but you can visit Disney World ... lovely spot for mouse vacations don't you know? No mouse traps or cats allowed in the place ... Company policy."

Bert took a deep breath. "Well, actually Uncle Thomas, we were thinking of a more permanent move. A few years anyway. We would like to go to the Oregon coast. Preferably the northwest corner."

Uncle Thomas raised his eyebrows. "Oregon you say? Goodness me! Why would you go there? It rains all the time, don't you know?"

Bert smiled at Mavis. "It's where we want to go, Uncle Thomas," she said.

Uncle Thomas twitched his whiskers. "I don't wish to sound patronizing, my dears. But Oregon?" He pointed to the map. "Look where it is! Almost as far north as Alaska. Your tails will freeze off in the winter."

Mavis laughed out loud. "Please, Uncle Thomas. It's much farther south. It's just north of California. Besides, Oregon winters are *much* warmer than St. Louis winters!"

Bert hastily intervened. "How much would it cost?"

Uncle Thomas gave a loud sniff. "MTI offers a variety of traveling options, Albert. It just depends on what you want to spend."

"What do we pay with?" Mavis asked.

Uncle Thomas seemed rather taken aback. "I would have thought that was quite obvious."

Mavis looked perplexed. "I don't understand, Uncle."

Uncle Thomas gave out a rather theatrical sigh. "Use your nose, my dear girl. Take a sniff for goodness sake."

"Cheese?" Bert gasped. "We have to pay in cheese?"

Uncle Thomas rolled his eyes. "Exactly. Cheese is the only currency I accept. Hard cheese, mind you. None of that mushy, soft, French stuff."

Uncle Thomas took a deep breath and a faraway look appeared in his eyes. "Nothing to beat a good bit of English cheddar. Travels very well and easy to divide up." He turned towards them. "Have you ever tried to slice up Brie? You have it all over you in no time. Disgusting stuff. Not worth a button."

Uncle Thomas pulled out a package of yellow colored papers

Bert and Mavis exchanged worried looks. Uncle Thomas' features softened.

"Buck up, you two. We have a special *Pioneer Package* for adventurous folk like you. It will be a piece of cake. Or should I say cheese?" He burst into a giggle of self-appreciation.

Mavis was still concerned. "The trip will take several days; do we have to carry food with us?"

Uncle Thomas's face positively beamed. "All part of the *Pioneer Package*, my dear girl." He pointed towards the map. "We have MTI agents in most of the cities in the U.S. They will make sure you have food for each stage of the journey and provide some overnight accommodation at transfer stations as necessary."

"But what happens when we get to Oregon?" asked Mavis. "It may take some time to find a home and adequate food supplies."

19

Uncle Thomas turned towards a small cavity in the wall and pulled out a package of yellow colored papers. "These will solve your problems. MTI travelers' cheeseks."

"You mean checks?" said Bert.

Uncle Thomas shook his head vigorously from side to side. "No, my dear chap. Cheeseks. Our human friends, to assist them in financial transactions, use checks. We use cheeseks to assist us in our cheese transactions. They can be made out for any amount from ounces to pounds and can be redeemed into cheese at any MTI agency in the country." He flicked through the sheaf of yellow papers. "This little package is worth five pounds of cheese. Imagine having to carry that all the way to Oregon."

Bert was impressed. "I can take one of these cheeseks to anyplace in the country and have it exchanged for cheese?"

"Only MTI agents, my dear boy." Uncle Thomas twirled his whiskers. "Mind you, the day will come when my cheeseks will find general acceptance." He straightened his shoulders. "Not just here in the United States, but worldwide." He lapsed into a thoughtful silence, looking far into an unseen distance. "London, Hong Kong, Berlin ... even Paris. One must not be narrow-minded when dealing internationally, must one? I'm sure the French are capable of producing a passable hard cheese." He sighed. "It would mean going metric of course."

Bert shook his head. "I'm really impressed, Uncle Thomas."

His uncle beamed. "Well, as you well know, Albert, I am not one to boast. Nevertheless, I do feel some sense of achievement." He twitched his whiskers. "I'm playing around with the idea of going into plastic currency, MTI Cheesa Credit Card. Cuts back on the paperwork. Saves the trees. Preserves the Ozone Layer. That sort of thing."

Bert gave a deep sigh. "It is all just wonderful, Uncle. But we may not be able to scrape together enough cheese to take us to Oregon."

His uncle smiled. "My dear Albert. You are family, after all. We can work out something to get you to Oregon. It's just a question of what's available and that information is in the MTI operation center. Follow me."

Chapter Three

Gorbi the Cat

Uncle Thomas swept out of sight through the door. Bert and Mavis scurried after him. They passed quickly through a series of dark, dusty tunnels and narrow openings, then passed through one more opening. Uncle Thomas stopped so suddenly that Mavis and Bert almost collided with him.

"Here we are. This is where it all happens, my dears. Yes, indeed."

Mavis and Bert took in their surroundings. It was very dark and there was little to see.

Uncle Thomas craned his neck to look upwards. He took a deep breath. "Ahoy there. Ian. Bill. Matt. Lower away."

Bert looked up. His eyes were growing accustomed to the dark. He could now see that they were standing beside a giant desk, just like the director had at the museum.

There was a creaking sound behind them. Bert looked over his shoulder. The office door was slowly opening and an ever-widening shaft of faint light fanned out across the room. A large, dark shape appeared against the backdrop of the dimly lit hallway.

Bert gave out a gasp of fear. It was a cat, a frightening large black cat.

"Run! Mavis! Uncle! Run!"

Mavis turned and froze. Bert began to push her back to the entrance.

"Steady on, old chap. Steady on." Uncle Thomas patted Bert reassuringly on the back. Bert turned. Uncle Thomas was smiling and making no attempt to escape. Bert looked towards the open door. There was no sign of a cat.

"Uncle. There was a cat. At the door. A large, black cat." The words tumbled out of Bert's mouth.

Uncle Thomas smiled. "That must have been Gorbi. Nothing to worry about, old chap."

"But it was a cat, Uncle ... I don't understand."

Uncle Thomas continued to smile, though now it was more like a smirk. "We reached *détente* with old Gorbi long, long ago, Albert."

"*Détente?*" Mavis was also puzzled.

"Yes, Mavis my dear ... *détente*. A mutual satisfaction treaty between us and Gorbi."

Bert shook his head in disbelief. "A treaty between mice and a cat?"

"He has to earn a living just like us, Albert. We all have to eat. Food is a great leveler."

"But a treaty? How does it operate?" said Mavis.

Uncle Thomas twitched his whiskers. "Very simply, my dear. Gorbi keeps an eye open for the security guards and warns us when they are in the vicinity. We supply Gorbi with fresh smoked salmon shipped in from the West Coast every week."

Mavis shook her head in disbelief. "How ever did you negotiate with a cat?"

Uncle Thomas shrugged his shoulders. "Quite a simple process, my dear. We just left a few samples of smoked salmon laying around for Gorbi to find. Didn't take him long to decide it tasted better than mice and was less exhausting. We do arrange a few cat and mouse chases to keep Gorbi's employers happy."

A box shaped object appeared out of the gloom above them and slowly descended to the floor. The bold print on the side of the box identified its origins: STERLING PAPER CLIPS.

Uncle Thomas ushered them aboard. "You both go first. My weight would overload the system."

Bert and Mavis looked reluctantly into the box. Four cords, one from each corner, were attached to a single paper clip, which was suspended to another cord stretching up into the darkness.

"Is this safe?" Mavis whispered as she climbed into the box.

Bert, climbing in next to her, forced a casual tone. "Of course it is. Uncle Thomas is not one for taking risks." But he wasn't too sure himself about the safety of the apparatus.

Seeing them safely aboard, Uncle Thomas stepped back and craned his neck to look upwards. "Okay, chaps. Take her up."

There was a whirring sound from above. The box jerked up from the floor and began a rapid ascent. Mavis and Bert clutched at the sides of the box as it made rather jerky progress upwards.

The whirring sound increased in volume as they ascended. Bert looked up. Shapes were taking form. The pace suddenly dropped off. Then Bert and Mavis saw the lifting mechanism. The cord was wrapped around a pencil, which was jammed into an electric sharpener. Suddenly they stopped.

The box swung to and fro, and Bert and Mavis clung to the sides. They were now level with the top of the desk. Three young mice appeared and pulled the box in until it rested on the desktop. Bert and Mavis wasted no time in disembarking, glad to have their feet on a solid foundation once more.

"Hurry along there, you chaps," sounded the faint voice of Uncle Thomas below.

The three mice moved quickly to take hold of the pencil. They pulled it clear of the sharpener and gradually lowered the box into the darkness below. The cord slackened as the box reached the floor. They jammed the end of the pencil once more into the sharpener. On a call from Uncle Thomas one of the mice flicked the switch, the electric motor whirred noisily, and soon Uncle Thomas joined them.

He beamed at Bert and Mavis. "How do you like our elevator?"

Bert smiled. "Very innovative, Uncle."

Uncle Thomas nodded his head. "We Brits do have something of a reputation for improvisation. Yes, indeed. There is another route up here, of course, but at my age I find this system less wearing on the old body."

He turned towards the three young mice. "Ian, Bill, Matt, this is your cousin Albert and his lovely wife Mavis."

There was a whirring sound from above.
The box jerked up from the floor and bagan a rapid ascent.

The three mice smiled and in unison responded. "Pleased to meet you, Albert and Mavis."

Bert and Mavis returned the greeting, struggling to keep straight faces.

Bert looked around. Apart from a few books, the desktop was sparse and uncluttered. A computer dominated the scene, the large monitor screen towering above them, shining in the dim light. Giant cables snaked out from the back and down into the darkness. At the base was a giant keyboard, rows of gray plastic keys marked with letters and numbers. Next to the keyboard was another, smaller piece. It was not much bigger than Bert, flat-sided and shell-shaped. There was one button on the top and a cable connected it to the computer. It had no markings. A couple of trays stacked with paper and the pencil sharpener completed the scant furnishings.

"What is this place, Uncle?" Bert asked.

"The office of one of the shipping clerks in the shipping company. Not quite executive standard as you see, but it is the brain center of Mouse Trips International." Uncle Thomas sighed. "I'm afraid the poor clerk gets in trouble from his supervisor for going through so many pencils, but there isn't much we can do about it."

Uncle Thomas turned to the three young mice. "Let's show your cousins our little operation lads. Chop, Chop!"

Chapter Four

Computer Mice

The three young mice scampered off. Ian went around the side of the computer, Bill went to the keyboard, and Matt positioned himself beside the shell shaped piece. "Power on, Ian," shouted Uncle Thomas. There was a clicking sound, and Bert and Mavis flinched as a loud humming vibrated the air around them.

"Switch on, Matt," Uncle Thomas called out.

Matt moved to the base, scrambled up beside the monitor, and pressed a button. Lights flickered and a jumble of numbers and letters raced across the screen.

"Key in, Bill." Uncle Thomas was obviously having fun.

Bill pushed down on a key, then scurried up to the topside of the board and pushed another key. The screen erupted into a flurry of colored images. Mavis gasped out loud in wonder. Bill pushed another key and columns of words flickered down the screen.

"Windows, Bill!" Uncle Thomas shouted.

Bert looked around quickly in confusion. There were no windows in the office. He glanced back at the monitor. Several overlapping columns of titles filled the screen.

Uncle Thomas nodded his head. "Okay chaps, let's get on the mouse."

Bert and Mavis looked around for another mouse, but the three cousins were now at the shell shaped object. Ian was on the left side and Bill took a position on the right. Matt stood between them, leaning over the rounded top.

Uncle Thomas saw that Mavis was puzzled. "That whatsit the boys are at is the *mouse*." He gave them a knowing wink and flashed a toothy grin. "That's what our human friends call it, don't you know? We should take it as a compliment, I suppose."

He turned back to the monitor and gave a grunt of satisfaction. "Here we go," he said, turning to his three helpers.

"Left a bit," he called out. The three young mice slid the mouse to the left.

Bert looked up at the screen. A bright little arrow was moving across it. As the mouse moved, so did the arrow.

"Now forward a bit. Stop. Left. Left. Stop!" Uncle Thomas waved his arm. "Press, Matt!"

Matt pressed hard down on the single button.

"Left. Left. Stop. Right; a bit more, chaps!" Uncle Thomas fired off instructions to the three assistants, sending them one way and then the other. They were beginning to breath heavily as they hauled and pushed their burden across the surface of the desk.

Bert and Mavis stared at the monitor; lists of names and dates moved across the screen as Matt punched keys.

"Stop! That's it!" Uncle Thomas's voice was high-pitched with excitement. Matt, about to push another key, quickly drew back, lost his balance, and fell down with a dramatic thud.

Uncle Thomas rolled his eyes and gave an impatient sigh. "Stop clowning around, Matt."

He stepped back to get a better view of the screen, nodding his head with satisfaction. "Ah! Here we are. Good. Good. Everyone relax."

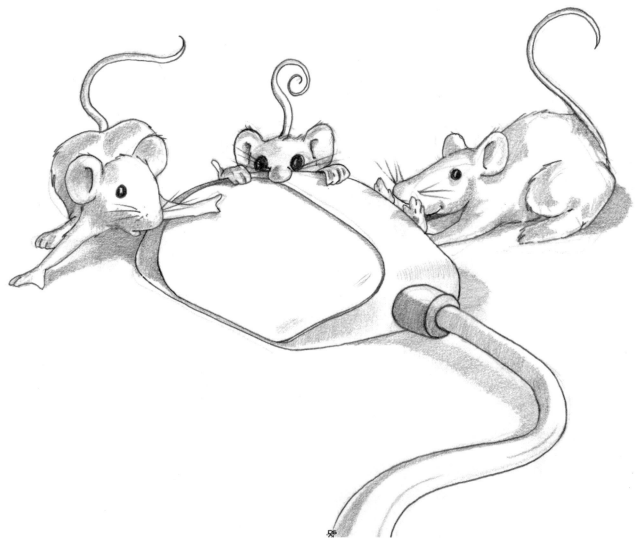

They were beginning to breathe heavily as they hauled and pushed their burden across the surface of the desk.

There was a muffled sigh from the mouse team. Exhausted, they slid down to sitting positions.

"It seems to be very hard work, Uncle," said Bert, as he viewed his weary cousins.

Uncle Thomas turned from his study of the monitor. "Yes, I suppose it is. I do feel quite drained some days ... the concentration, you know? The technology gets better all the time, of course. We are much faster now. That mouse is only half the size of the last model." He turned back to his study of the monitor screen.

"What are these lists, Uncle?" asked Bert.

"Transportation and delivery schedules for this month, my dear chap." He twitched his whiskers. "Shows all the destinations and dates for goods being delivered all over the country." He turned and smiled. "Now let us see what we have for the jolly old West Coast."

Uncle Thomas snapped out a few more commands and more lists flickered across the screen. "Ah hah! Here we are. Crate of crockery for Seattle on the 14th." He turned to Mavis and Bert. "Very smooth trip. Handle with care. Fragile. That sort of thing. Very smooth, yes indeed."

"Too far north, Uncle." said Bert, apologetically.

Uncle Thomas twitched his whiskers and turned back to the screen. "Box of tee shirts to Walla Walla on the 17th ."

Bert and Mavis exchanged excited looks

"Walla Walla?" Mavis questioned. "I thought that was an onion."

Uncle Thomas sighed. "Yes, yes, my dear," he said impatiently. "That's where they grow the blessed things." He continued to study the screen.

"Wait a minute. By Jove, I think we have it!" A broad smile once more graced his features. "A box of kites for Cannon Beach. Via Portland, Oregon."

Bert and Mavis exchanged excited looks. "That will be perfect, Uncle Thomas," said Bert as he gave Mavis a hug. "Just perfect."

Chapter Five

Cannon Beach

The truck stopped, as it had done many times before, the rumble of the roll-up door followed by the clump of heavy feet. Inside the kite box, Bert and Mavis waited with baited breath. Was this it, at last? Previous disappointments had long since dulled the edge of their excitement, but the fluttery feeling in their stomachs was still there. Their supply of cheese was very low and they had lost all sense of time.

A sudden jolt sent them sprawling. The kite box had been lifted up. They rolled to and fro as it was carried out of the truck. Some more bumps and jolts, the creak of a rusty door hinge, more jolting, and then a final jarring and scraping of the bottom of the box along some flat surface. They could hear muffled voices. Then silence.

They waited for some time before venturing out of the kite box into the surrounding darkness. Then, as their eyes adjusted, they began to pick out details of their surroundings.

It was in a large room, with kites of all shapes and sizes hanging from the walls. Larger kites hung from the ceiling beams, their colored tail ribbons fluttering in drafts of cold air that came from the far end of the room. They instinctively followed the draft to a large door. There was a gap between the door and the floor large enough to allow them to slip out into the chilly night.

As their eyes adjusted, they began to pick out details of their surroundings.

The wind that rustled overhead carried sounds strange to their city ears. Rushing, crashing, roaring sounds. Bert looked at Mavis and swallowed hard. "It's the sea, Mavis. The Pacific Ocean."

They ran side by side through the dark, empty streets, the sound of breaking surf getting louder with every stride. Turning off onto a side street, they soon left the paved asphalt behind and were winding through tall, rough grass waving in the stiffening breeze. The ground below them became softer with each step and the grass began to thin out. Their feet sank into sand, a sensation new to both of them and they were giddy with excitement.

When they broke clear from the grass, Bert and Mavis stopped in their tracks. It was still quite dark, but the roaring of the distant surf was louder than ever.

"It's the beach, Mavis," said Bert in a reverent whisper. "Let's keep going."

Mavis shook her head vigorously. "I don't think we should, Bert. We don't know what's out there," she said. "Let's wait till it gets lighter."

Bert reluctantly agreed. They found a small hollow in the grass that sheltered them from the wind and settled down as best they could until dawn. For Bert, the passage of time stretched out into a restless eternity, but soon the gray light of morning crept into the eastern sky.

They were giddy with excitement.

Mavis had drifted off into a peaceful sleep, and impatient though he was, Bert was reluctant to disturb her. It had been an exhausting trip for both of them, but was especially so for an expectant mother.

The wind had dropped and the tall grass above them rustled gently in the light breeze. The sky grew brighter by the minute, but the sun had not yet appeared. Bert crept forward to the edge of the grass. A cover of mist blanketed the beach and muffled the roar of the invisible surf.

Bert shook Mavis gently. "Time to go, Mavis."

Mavis sleepily arose. She pushed aside some blades of grass and looked out onto the beach. The mist had risen slightly, forming a fuzzy, gray ceiling above the brown expanse of the sand.

"It's so big, Bert," she said, shivering with a mixture of awe and fear.

Bert was not dismayed. "It's not so big. It's the mist that makes it seem so." He looked to the east and gave a shout of satisfaction. "Look! The sun."

Mavis turned. A dull white orb had appeared on the horizon. Almost immediately the morning mist began to disperse.

Bert stepped out onto the beach. "Come on, Mavis. Let's run out there and back before people start to come."

Mavis pushed aside her fears and set off excitedly after him. The fog bank was now rolling back out to sea, and the frothing white line of the breaking surf had appeared. The sun had changed from white to yellow. As they hurried towards the sea, the sand made a strange squeaking noise under their feet. Bert giggled in delight. "Listen Mavis, it's just like Lewis and Clark described in their diaries. The squeaking sand. Isn't it great?"

Mavis forced a brave smile. It *was* great; their long journey was finally over. But it was so new, so different than anything they had ever seen before. She stared ahead. A large, dark shape had begun to materialize. It rose out of the sea, towering up until it vanished into the rising ceiling of the fog.

"What's that Bert?" she gasped.

"It's just a big rock, Mavis. Come on, we are almost there." Bert charged ahead.

As Mavis followed, staring ahead at the large tower, she banged into the sharp edge of a broken shell. "Ouch," she yelled, sitting down and licking her foot. Bert came running back.

"Are you alright, Mavis?"

Mavis climbed back onto her feet, brushing the sand off. "Yes ... I'm fine, but ... "

A distant screeching sound interrupted her. It was coming from the giant rock, its cone shaped top now showing through the vanishing mist. White shapes appeared on its black surface. The screeching increased in volume.

Mavis turned to Bert. He was staring up at the rock.

"What is it Bert?" she whispered.

"I think it could ... " Bert's words died as one of the white objects launched itself from the face of the rock. It was followed by another, then several more.

Bert reacted quickly. "Run, Mavis! Run before they spot us. Gulls! Those are gulls!"

Mavis's heart leapt into her mouth, but she wasted no time and started to run away from the sea. The sun had now broken clear of the mist and burned brightly into their eyes.

Bert stayed behind Mavis. He cast a quick glance over his shoulder. Scores of gulls were swooping and soaring around the rock. Others were gliding down towards the beach.

Breathing heavily he turned back. The safe haven of the grassy dune seemed miles away. A higher pitched screech pierced the air behind him. He cast another fearful look behind. One of the gulls was swooping down towards them. Bert's heart froze. They had been spotted.

There was a rush of air behind. Bert swerved to the side. A giant, white shape flashed past him; webbed feet scraped across the sand and the gull soared up into the sun.

Mavis was now some distance away from Bert. She was close to the safety of the grass, but she stopped to turn around and look for Bert. "Come on, Bert, come on!" she cried, as he ran towards her. A shadow darkened the sand. Bert looked up above. A gull was swooping towards Mavis.

Mavis followed his gaze up and saw the gull. "Bert! Bert!" Her desperate cry pierced his heart. The gull swooped low over her then banked steeply for the attack.

Bert knew there was only one thing to do. He turned sharply and started to run. The gull was now skimming low towards Mavis.

Bert raced to get between Mavis and the attacker.

"Run, Mavis, Run!"

There was a deafening sound as a giant beak clamped around his rear leg. Wings beat around him and the beach began to fall below as the gull screeched into the sky. As he slipped into unconsciousness, the last thing he saw far below was the tiny shape of Mavis vanishing into the grass.

CHAPTER SIX

ANGUS, M.D.

Mavis, from the security of the tall spiky grass, screamed in grief as the gull soared up with Bert clutched in its beak. Suddenly another gull attacked the first. Bert, loosed by the first gull, dropped like a stone through a sky filled with swooping, shrieking birds. One caught him just short of the ground then almost immediately collided with another gull. Bert's limp shape was thrown clear and vanished from her view.

Mavis sobbing with despair ran through the grass. She found Bert crumpled on top of broken blades of grass. But through her tears and her panic, she saw that he was still breathing. She gave a gasp of relief. He was alive.

Bert groaned slightly. There was a noise behind her. Mavis whirled around to see a small gathering of mice.

There was no better mouse doctor than old Angus

The west coast mice had darker fur than Mavis and Bert, and they spoke with a softer accent; but their outpouring of support diminished their differences. They wove a stretcher out of grass to carry Bert to medical attention in the basement of the local drug store, where Mavis and Bert first met Angus, M.D.

The mouse doctor for the local community, Angus had the same light fur as Mavis and Bert, but spoke with the rolling brogue of his Scottish homeland. He had learned his skills as a young mouse in the basement of Edinburgh Royal Infirmary. There was no better mouse doctor than old Angus.

Under his care Bert made a rapid, though not complete, recovery. He had fractured his left leg so badly that he would have a decided limp for the rest of his life.

Their dramatic arrival in Cannon Beach helped them find a rapid degree of acceptance in the local mouse community. They soon found a cozy home behind a stack of old bibles in the cellar of a small Presbyterian Church situated at the south end of the town. Bert seemed to have lost all interest in dipping his feet in the Pacific Ocean, and as far as Mavis was concerned, the further away from the sea they were, the better.

The community quickly learned of Bert and Mavis's museum education. He was offered a teaching position at the community school. Bert was well liked by the students and the faculty. His injured leg affected his posture to such a degree that he soon earned the nickname *Pisa,* after the famous Italian leaning tower.

Mavis, meanwhile, prepared for the new arrival. One night, Mavis and Bert were relaxing in their cozy living room. Mavis put down her knitting. "What shall we call the baby, Bert?"

Bert looked up over the newspaper. "Well, I've been thinking about that. It would be good to recognize why we're here. I think either Lewis or Clark would be a great name."

Mavis rolled her eyes. "What if it's a girl, Bert?"

Bert put on a patient smile. "Come on, Mavis. Look at our family history. I have six brothers, you have four brothers and all our cousins are male. It's in the genes."

"Well, not *everyone* is male, Bert," Mavis said indignantly. "I'm not."

Bert leaned forward and kissed her on the cheek. "And for that, I'm very grateful."

But Mavis was not amused. "Just because our families are overloaded with males doesn't prove anything.

Bert shook his head. "No, no, Mavis! It just proves how unique you really are."

Mavis's expression softened a bit. "Don't start buttering me up, Bert. Just you wait and see. I think it will be a girl."

"And hopefully she'll be every bit as feisty as her mother," Bert said, managing to get his newspaper up just in time to deflect the ball of wool.

As it turned out, they were both right. A few weeks later, Mavis did indeed give birth to a fine, healthy baby boy, and, much to everyone's surprise, a fine, healthy baby girl. And in keeping with Bert's idea, the twins were named *Louise* and Clark, in honor of their parents' adventurous journey.

The twins grew quickly. But in spite of the fact that they were twins, they were different in many ways. Clark was studious and showed great interest in the business of the church. From the safe vantage of the organ loft, he would listen in on Sunday services, paying particular attention to the Reverend Finley's eloquent sermons. He took some pride in his general Bible knowledge, but soon learned that repeating scriptures he found interesting to his peers was no guarantee for cementing friendships. Eventually his strident efforts to impress earned him a nickname: 'Clackety Clack' or 'Clack' for short.

Louise, on the other hand, was no academic and always impatient for adventure. Restless and always on the go, *action first and thought later* became her trademark in the community. Initially, it brought her some cautious respect from peers and elders. Then one night, she was asked to join a scavenging party that was paying a daring, after-hours visit to the general store. The gathering of various, tasty treats was well under way when Louise pulled an apple from the bottom row of a giant pyramid display. The subsequent avalanche of fruit wrought havoc amongst the mice party and alerted the store cat. The panic-stricken and humiliating retreat from the store deflated the egos of the party leaders and Louise suffered the consequences. One of the leaders commented bitterly that the youngster had a nut loose and Louise's peers picked up on that very quickly. From then on she also had a nickname: 'Loose Nut' or 'Loose' for short.

Time passed, but the nicknames Loose and Clack did not. The twins became something of a joke in the community and their circle of friends was small. In spite of their differences, they turned more and more to each other for company and support, and the twins became best friends as well as brother and sister.

As for Bert and Mavis, their circle of acquaintances was quite large. But their eastern accents and lighter fur seemed to be a barrier to forming deep, lasting relationships, and in the close-knit community, it would be a long time before Bert and Mavis would be anything other than newcomers. It was no surprise that their only truly close friend was a fellow newcomer, Dr. Angus.

Angus was often homesick for Scotland and when Bert introduced him to Mouse Trips International, he was able to make his first visit home in several years. These became annual trips and his travel schedule never varied: eastward to Scotland in a box of Tillamook Cheese and a return trip to Cannon Beach in a crate of whisky. He said it was difficult to decide which leg of the journey was the most enjoyable.

Louise and Clark always enjoyed visiting Angus at his little shop in the pharmacy basement. There he kept little boxes of medicines that he had managed to gather from the storage room. Often, they would help him break the giant, round slabs of aspirin into portions suitable for mice, and he would tell them tales of Scotland and recite poetry by his favorite Scottish bard Robert Burns, or as Angus called him, 'Rabbie' Burns.

They could not understand all of the words but enjoyed the performances. Angus's favorite Burns poem was *To a Mouse,* insisting that the mouse in question was his great-great-grandfather, Angus MacDonald of Ayr. Angus's Scottish brogue made the word mouse sound like moose. The twins would tease him and ask where his antlers were. His favorite line in the poem was 'The best laid schemes o' mice an' men gang aft agley.'

Thus, the arrival of Bert and Mavis also turned out to be the gift of a family for Angus. The lonely Scottish doctor forged his own close-knit unit with the newcomers from St. Louis.

Chapter Seven

The Beach

The beach was off-limits to all the youngsters in the mice community, but even more so for Louise and Clark. Mavis had urgently repeated her warning many times, telling in great detail the incident with the gulls. Though their father never brought up the subject, they could not help but notice that he never traveled any route that took him anywhere near the seashore. But for some youngsters the attraction of the unknown can be strong and so it was for Louise.

One day, on the way back from an after-hours class at school, the twins passed close to a long sand dune. The evening breeze that wafted through the tall, rough grass carried the muffled roar of the distant surf and the pungent smell of salt water and seaweed.

"Let's go and have a look," said Louise, eyes wide with anticipation.

Clark shook his head. "You know what Mom told us, Louise. It's dangerous. The gulls."

"We can have a quick look. What harm could that do?"

Clark took a deep breath. "Matthew 19, verse 19. Honor your father and your mother."

Louise rolled her eyes. "I do honor Mom and Dad ... What's that got to do with taking a peek at the beach?"

"They told us to keep clear of the beach."

Louise cut in. "They wouldn't want us to go to the moon either, but they let us look at it. I just want to get close enough to see the beach, that's all."

Clark searched for a weakness in the analogy but couldn't find one. Louise had already started up the lower slope of the dune.

Clark hesitated, looked all around for a moment, then started after his sister. Louise was already weaving through the tall grass when Clark caught up with her, puffing from running through sand. The sound of the surf grew louder than ever.

Louise stopped suddenly and Clark almost fell over her. "Geez, Louise," he started in annoyance — until he saw why his sister had stopped.

The beach. The enormous beach. Its size was way beyond all Clark's imaginings, stretching out endlessly to the right and to the left. Far ahead it terminated in a foaming, turbulent, white line of surf. Beyond the surf, giant rocks jutted up into the blue sky. One in particular rose high above the others. Hundreds of birds of all shapes and sizes zoomed and fluttered around its top creating a living halo of white and brown. The sun hung low in the western sky, casting a rippling band of gold across the waves to the beach. A few people walked along the shore, some with dogs; a rider on a horse galloped noiselessly by.

Even Louise was impressed with the grandeur of it all. "Have you ever seen anything so awesome, Clark?" she whispered, eyes wide.

Clark shook his head slowly.

Louise suddenly cocked her head to one side.

"What is it?" whispered Clark.

"Listen. Don't you hear something?" countered Louise.

Clark strained his ears. At first all he could hear above the distant roar of the surf and the rustle of the wind-tossed grass was the beating of his heart. Then he began to detect something else. The wind changed direction and the sound became clearer. It was someone singing, a familiar voice singing.

"*My love is like a red, red rose that's newly sprung in June. Oh my love is like a melody that ...*" A gust of wind blew the remaining words away.

Louise started to creep through the grass in the direction of the mysterious singer. Clark cautiously followed in the rear.

The singing grew louder. "*... Till all the years run dry, my dear. Till all the years run dry ... I will ...*"

Then they saw the singer, sitting on a tuft of moss overlooking the beach.

"Angus, is that you?" Louise called out.

The singing suddenly stopped and the mouse turned around. Angus was holding a small, glass medicine bottle, full of a gold colored liquid. He quickly stuck a small cork into the bottle and hid it out of sight.

"Well, goodness, gracious me. It's the terrible twins. Come and sit yourselves down." Angus's Scottish brogue was stronger than usual.

"What are you doing, Angus?" questioned Louise, a mischievous grin on her face.

Angus cleared his throat rather loudly. "Just came to see the sunset, lassie. This is my favorite view. Reminds me of home a wee bit."

"It is a nice beach," said Clark quickly as he cast a disapproving look at his sister.

"Och, it's not just the beach. It's the Haystack that makes it so special."

Louise look puzzled. "I don't see any haystacks."

Angus smiled. "That's what the human people call the big rock." He sniffed. "I thought teacher's bairns would know that."

Clark nodded his head. "I see ... it's shaped like a haystack."

The old mouse nodded. "Aye. It reminds me of the Bass Rock."

"Is that in Edinburgh?" asked Louise.

Angus shook his head. "No. It's in a wee, seaside town not far from Edinburgh, called North Berwick. It's where I used to go on my summer holidays when I was a youngster." He went quiet for a few seconds. "Of course the Bass Rock is a lot bigger ... but covered with gulls and the like, just like the Haystack."

Louise turned to watch the giant birds swooping and soaring above the massive rock. "Have any mice ever gone out to the Haystack, Angus?"

Angus shook his head slowly. "None that ever came back lassie." He turned with a quiet smile.

It's the Haystack that makes it so special

"Of course your mum and dad almost made it once."

Louise kicked some sand with her feet. "Some kids in my class say that Dad is frightened of the beach." She glanced up at Angus. "Is that true?"

Angus did not answer right away, staring out to sea. "I wouldnae blame him for that, lassie. He had a terrible experience. It was a miracle he survived."

"They say it was stupid what he tried to do," said Clark.

Angus sighed and got to his feet. "Not stupid lad. Maybe a wee bit ignorant, that's all. Your Dad was trying to achieve a great ambition. He just didn't know what he was up against." He dusted some sand off his coat. "But at the end of it all, he risked his life to save your mother ... and you wouldnae be here talking about it but for that." He turned to leave. "You better be getting off home before its dark. I'll be seeing you."

Angus headed off down the slope and disappeared into the dense grass.

CHAPTER EIGHT

ON THE WINGS OF EAGLES

Louise and Clark looked back towards the sea. The sun had sunk halfway into the ocean and the sky was turning magnificent shades of red, pink, and purple. They wasted no more time and scampered down the hill after Angus.

From that time on the twins would make frequent visits to the dune, and from the safe vantage point of the tall grass, they would view the pageant of life that the advent of spring and summer revealed. Every visit would show more and more beachcombers, horse riders, dog walkers, sunbathers, and bicyclists. But the biggest fascination for both Louise and Clark were the kites. Kites of all shapes and sizes, all colors and patterns. Small kites, large kites, single kites, double kites, and even multiple kites linked together. They swept low across the beach and soared high in the sky, driving away the seabirds that had been attracted by the tempting tidbits of the many picnickers.

One time they had to duck for safety as an aerobatic kite swept through the grass above them, its fabric fluttering, then zoomed up into the heavens, its long multicolored tail ribbons trailing gracefully behind.

"Wouldn't it be magic to fly like that?" gasped Louise as she watched.

Clark shook his head. "Mice can't fly, Louise. We're not meant to fly."

Louise gave an exasperated groan. "Don't be such a wet blanket, Clark."

Clark gave a loud sniff. "If God wanted us to fly He would have given us wings."

"What about humans? They don't have wings and they fly. And anyway where does it say we can't fly in the Bible?"

Clark pondered the question for a moment. "It must be there somewhere. Just can't think where at the moment, but it's obvious to anyone with any common sense."

This taunt was like a gauntlet being thrown down for Louise. She proceeded to ask her father questions about flight. Bert, of course, was very well up on the subject, having once studied a Wright Brothers exhibition at the museum back in St. Louis.

Bert was happy to pass on his knowledge of the theory of flight. He and Mavis were encouraged that Louise should show such an interest in learning which had been noticeably lacking up till then.

Louise then had a stroke of good fortune when she and Clark visited the basement of the town's toyshop. They came upon a discarded plan for a model glider, some balsa wood, and a half-used tube of cement. The discovery seemed like fate to Louise. The audacity of her plans quickly restored her reputation amongst her classmates at school. Many, including Clark, even volunteered to help.

The assembly of the glider was carried out in an old, abandoned garden shed, well away from the eyes and ears of parents. As the craft took shape it was soon dubbed, *The Spirit of St Loose*.

Days stretched into weeks and the first faint murmurs of ridicule could be heard from the uninvolved. But the dedicated little team of glider builders pressed on until the job was done. Louise and Clark drew straws to be the pilot on the first flight. Louise was the winner, but Clark did not appear to be overly disappointed.

The site for the maiden flight was chosen with great care. Louise found a quiet little meadow, which sloped gently down to a small pond. Scores of last minute enthusiasts helped drag the glider to its launching position. The crowd of youngsters that gathered to view this historic moment were generally impressed.

"Gosh, do you think Louise could be another Amelia Earhart?" whispered one of Louise's classmates.

"It's just like Howard Hughes's *Spruce Goose*," another one said.

"*Loose* Goose is more like it," commented a more cynical spectator after viewing the glider's structure.

The launching system was simple. Two stakes were buried in the soft soil with a giant rubber band slung between them. A hook on the underside of the glider's nose was slipped over the band. Louise climbed into the cockpit with impressive dignity.

A score or so of mice took hold of the tail and fuselage and began to haul it back up the slope. The rubber band stretched and stretched. As its tension increased, more mice joined in to help. A small length of string attached to the glider's tail was tied to a third stake, and the mice were relieved of the strain.

All was now ready. A small sliver of sharp glass was held over the tail string by one mouse who looked to Louise for the signal. Silence fell on the crowd.

Clark insisted that a short scripture reading was appropriate. Louise, getting steadily more nervous, readily agreed. Clark chose Isaiah 40, verse 31. " '*Those who hope in the Lord will renew their strength. They will soar on wings like eagles. They shall ...*"

Even as he spoke there were ominous creaking sounds coming from the stressed frame of the glider. Louise was looking more anxious than ever. She turned to the mouse with the glass splinter still poised over the string.

"Cut on the count of three," she shouted out before crouching low in the cockpit, teeth clenched.

The excited crowd took up the count. "One ... Two ..."

With a loud crack, part of the tail section broke away.

And that was as far as they got. With a loud crack, part of the tail section broke away and the rest of the glider was catapulted high into the air.

A shocked gasp erupted from the crowd as the damaged glider, with Louise in the cockpit, reached its peak altitude, fell back towards the earth, and smashed through the tall rushes that grew on the edge of the pond. Another gasp rose up from the multitude followed by an eerie quiet. They stared in stunned silence at the ever-widening ripples on the empty surface of the pond.

Then there was a sudden rush of air bubbles on the surface of the pond and a head popped into view. It was Louise. The spell of silence was broken, and the mice, with Clark leading, rushed to the rescue.

Louise was dragged out of the cockpit, somewhat dazed. Clark fanned her face with a cloverleaf. Louise stared up at the sea of faces crowding over her. She smiled in a confused sort of way. "Did I make it?"

There was a moment of silence, and then somebody laughed. Then another joined in, and another. Laughter swept through the crowd like the wind through a field of wheat.

Louise learned that fame can be fleeting and hero worship can quickly change to scoffing. The disillusioned team of glider builders, along with the rest of the crowd, headed home, and Louise and Clark were left alone.

"I told you there wasn't enough cement," said Clark. "You needed a whole tube. Nobody builds a glider with a half empty tube."

Louise, still trying to dislodge water from her ears, was in no mood to receive belated advice.

"If you had chosen a shorter scripture reading it would have been fine," she snapped back. "It didn't need to be a sermon."

Clark was huffed. "You should be more thankful."

Louise looked at the nose section still floating in the pond. "I suppose so," she sighed. "I wish we had kept it a secret. The Wright Brothers didn't have a big crowd watching them the first time."

Clark's heart was softened. "It was pretty impressive, Louise. You did fly higher than any other mouse. If you had been killed you would have been a hero." He gave a shy smile. "I would rather have a living sister, even if she is a bit nutty."

Louise raised her eyes to meet her brother's. She cleared her throat. "We did put on a show didn't we?" she said, grinning broadly.

Clark grinned back. "Yes, we did. It was a magnificent failure!" The two burst into laughter and arm in arm, they headed home.

CHAPTER NINE

THE ELECTION

A month or so later the headmaster of Cannon Beach Mice High School retired and Bert was one of two candidates being considered for filling the vacancy. Bert's opponent Basil, another teacher at the high school, was younger and from California. Though not a native of the area, Basil had a flashy, gregarious style, which had wide appeal in the community.

Even though Bert was well respected for his knowledge and teaching ability, he was still regarded as a foreigner from the east. His self-effacing manner was mistaken by some members of the community as a sign of haughtiness, by some as a lack of confidence.

The school board decided that the choice of the new headmaster should be handled by a democratic election. Polling day was set for the following month.

Supporters of both candidates organized campaigns to canvass the community. Several wine and cheese parties were held and the political jingles *Make it a Cert with Bert* and *Let's Dazzle with Basil* were seen and heard everywhere.

Polls carried out by the local mice news service indicated a close contest after the first two weeks. Then the easygoing nature of the election began to change. Basil's supporters initiated a smear campaign, concentrating on the local mistrust of anyone east of the Rockies.

Basil took the lead in the polls, but Bert would not allow his supporters to follow negative campaigning. Instead, they emphasized his outstanding academic background and the excellent grades his students achieved. Support in the community was restored, and with a week to go he had drawn level with Basil.

Then his opponents introduced a more subtle campaign strategy. Bert's teaching abilities were not in question. But his emotional capacity to handle the stress and strain of headmaster's duties was another matter. The traumatic experience of his arrival at Cannon Beach had left permanent scars on his body and his spirit. Better to preserve his service to the community as an excellent teacher than to destroy him with the pressures of leadership, his opponents said.

This new ploy was immediately successful and once more Bert's campaign began to flounder. Bert himself began to suffer severe headaches. He was directed by Dr. Angus to rest and avoid public meetings. The election became, for all intents and purposes, a one-mouse race.

Just a few days before the election, Louise and Clark were playing hide and seek in the long grass. They overheard a conversation between Angus and their mother at the entrance to their church basement home. Angus had been paying a visit to Bert, who was once more confined to bed.

"Thanks for coming so quickly, Angus." There was a tremor in their mother's voice.

"Och, don't mention it, lass ... just try and keep him resting as best you can. He's going to be fine."

"Is it serious, Angus? What's wrong with him?"

"It's not serious, Mavis, I assure you of that. There is nothing physically wrong with the lad."

"Is it all this election business then?"

Angus cleared his throat. "That may have triggered it. But I don't believe it is the root of his problem, lass."

"Are you saying it's all in his head?" said Mavis sharply.

Angus cleared his throat once more. "You must have seen the change in him. He's not the same chap he was."

There was a moment of silence. "Yes ... I suppose you're right Angus. He has changed. He was always so good with the twins. Showing them how to do things. Playing with them. Now he seems so distant at times. Even to me. I know he loves us. But ..." Her voice broke in mid sentence. A quiet sobbing drifted through to the grass where Louise and Clark sat. They exchanged embarrassed looks; Louise blinked away a tear before Clark could notice.

The crying stopped. "Is there nothing we can do Angus?"

"Medicine has its limitations, lass. But I'm sure it all goes back to that day on the beach. Bert was about to achieve one of his great ambitions that morning when you tried to reach the ocean. He was so close. Till that gull got him. It was a very traumatic experience, Mavis. All the confidence of youth was knocked out of him that day. And after what he went through who can blame him?" Angus was silent for a moment. "The stress of this election nonsense has brought it all back. Some part of his spirit was left on the beach that day, lass. I do believe that if Bert could splash his face in the Pacific Ocean, his headaches would disappear."

Mavis and Angus began to stroll away from the church, out of earshot, leaving a bewildered and dismayed Louise and Clark sitting quietly in the grass.

CHAPTER TEN

THE MISSION

Later that same day Louise and Clark sat together in the long grass of the sand dune, looking out onto the beach and the looming mass of Haystack Rock. The sun was slipping steadily towards the horizon watched by only a few remaining people; most of the visitors had long since headed home for their evening meal.

The twins were silent. The conversation between Dr. Angus and their mother had left them with much to think about. At last, Clark spoke. "If we could only get Dad to the ocean. You heard Dr. Angus? He said it would make Dad well again."

Louise shrugged. "But that wouldn't work out. Dad won't go near the beach. You know that." She absentmindedly kicked at the sand with her feet, wincing with pain as she struck something hard. She began to brush the sand away from the object.

Clark sighed. "You're right of course. If only we could bring the ocean to him."

What are you thinking, Louise?

Louise was still digging the sand from a shiny and clear object. It was a small, empty, glass bottle with a little loop of string attached to its neck. Clark looked across. "That's Dr. Angus's bottle, isn't it?"

Louise managed a wry smile. Yes. He must have hid it that day we saw him." She picked up the empty bottle, pulled the little cork out with her teeth, and sniffed.

"Phew ..." She dropped it immediately. "What a pong."

Suddenly, Louise sat up. Her eyes widened. "Wait a minute!"

"What's wrong?" said Clark anxiously.

"What you said a minute ago." Louise's eyes sparkled with excitement.

"What did I say?" Clark was puzzled.

"About bringing the ocean to Dad," said Louise.

Clark shook his head. "Don't be ridiculous. How can we do that?"

Louise lifted up the small glass bottle. "With this."

Clark was puzzled. "What are you thinking, Louise?"

Louise looked towards the setting sun, which was now tinting the sky with red.

"When it gets dark, we can take the bottle down to the ocean, fill it up, and bring it back to Dad." She grinned broadly. "Then he could splash his face in the Pacific Ocean. Just like Dr. Angus said. And he would get his health back."

Clark looked from Louise to the bottle, then towards the now dark shape of the Haystack. He looked at his sister and swallowed hard. "I suppose we should at least try. For Dad's sake."

Louise rammed the small cork back into the bottle and hung the loop of string over her head. She looked towards the sea. The sun was resting on the horizon. "Once it gets dark, we go."

CHAPTER ELEVEN

THE HAYSTACK ROCK

Louise and Clark waited until the sun had completely disappeared and stars began appearing in the darkening heavens. They set off across the sand towards the still visible dark shadowy shape of the Haystack. It was to be their landmark to ensure they did not stray too far from a direct route to the ocean and for the return journey. The temperature was dropping rapidly and they stopped occasionally to listen through the background rush of the surf for any signs of danger. In a surprisingly short time they reached the foaming, white ocean surf.

Their anxiety somewhat subdued the elation of the moment. "Let's just fill this thing and get on home," said Clark.

The tide was coming in and their first efforts to fill the bottle saw them swept off their feet by the foaming, surging surf. "This is a lot harder than I thought it would be," sputtered Louise, her mouth full of ocean water. They retrieved the bottle and tried again. Once more they were sent head over heels by the churning water and had to scramble to safety against the drag of the retreating surf.

Finally, when the bottle was three quarters full, they decided that was enough. Louise stuffed the cork back into the bottle and slung it around her neck.

The twins shook the seawater out of their ears and took a moment to get their breath back. "We did it, Clark. We made it to the Pacific Ocean for Dad!" shouted Louise in triumph.

"We sure did," grinned Clark. "Guess you're not so crazy, after all." They set off on their return journey across the dark, flat expanse of the beach.

But as they scampered across the cool surface of the sand, lights appeared further down the beach. They could hear a muffled roaring sound, getting louder as the lights grew bigger. The light beams swept erratically across the sand.

Louise and Clark changed their direction to escape the advancing lights but to no avail. One beam caught them full on. They could hear people shouting above the roaring sound. A large motorbike cut right in front of the running mice covering them with sand and filling their nostrils with pungent fumes. Temporarily blinded and choking with the smoke, both mice stopped in their tracks. Another light picked them out and the machine came straight for them.

"Back to the rocks!" shouted Louise and started to run, followed by a panic stricken Clark. Two beams of light now chased after them and the roaring sound was getting louder by the second.

They ran a zigzag course to escape from their hunters, but the bikes were almost upon them. Clark stumbled for several steps, then got his balance back. Suddenly they were running between some small rocks, then larger ones.

The roaring increased and a hail of sand rained down on the fleeing mice. Clark looked back over his shoulder. The lights were turning away, back along the beach. Louise had stopped and stood gasping for breath. Clark dropped to the sand beside her wheezing.

The erratic beams of light continued to jerk back and forward across the beach, the roaring of the engines fading against the rushing sound of the tide. The jerking lights headed back along the beach and vanished out of sight.

Louise and Clark changed their direction to escape the advancing lights but to no avail.

The two mice sat for some time until their nerves calmed down a bit. Louise at last got to her feet. "Let's go, Clark. Mom and Dad will be getting worried."

Clark gave a weary nod and pulled himself up onto his feet.

They started back towards the open beach. They had only gone a short distance when Louise suddenly halted and turned her head to listen.

"What is it?" Clark whispered.

"Listen. Listen to the sound of the surf," said Louise quietly.

Clark listened but could detect nothing different. "What of it?"

"It's between us and the open beach, that's what."

Clark listened again. He swallowed hard and turned to look at Louise. Suddenly seawater swirled around their feet.

"We're cut off!" yelled Louise. "The sea is all around us. We have to get higher. Quickly, Clark, quickly!"

They scrambled back through the rocks. The seawater lapped around their feet as they climbed higher onto a big rock. The sea came rushing up behind them. They climbed higher still. Clark was thinking of the seabirds that were sleeping high atop the Haystack. He was grateful for the darkness.

At last they reached a large shelf of rock and the seawater stopped rising. Louise looked down at the surface of the water swirling around a few feet below them. "That's blown it. We will have to wait till the tide turns. We are stuck here for the night."

Clark sighed, "Mom and Dad will be really worried."

Louise shrugged. "What else can we do?"

Clark shivered. A chill breeze had sprung up. "I should have known better than to go with you. The whole idea was crazy from the start. I need my head examined."

Louise rolled her eyes but did not respond. She looked around. "Let's get into one of these holes in the rock. We can't spend the night out in this wind. It will freeze our tails off."

They found a reasonably cozy little hole, snuggled into one another, and settled down for the night. The combined heat from their bodies eased the chill in their bones, and exhausted by events, they drifted off to sleep.

Later that evening a worried Mavis arrived at Angus's home looking for Louise and Clark. He and some friends scattered throughout the community to search for the missing twins. When they were no where to be found, Mavis had at last to break the news to Bert. He immediately got up from his bed and joined the search. It went on through the night and with the approach of dawn there was still no news.

In the gray light of morning, Angus, following a hunch, paid a visit to the grass-covered dune. He found the trails of two mice heading off across the beach until they vanished from his view. A few people had begun to stroll across the beach and hundreds of seabirds soared around the Haystack. But there was no sign of Louise and Clark.

Chapter Twelve

The Crabs

Clark woke with a start. He blinked in the dim, early morning light. Above the constant surge of the ocean he heard sounds ... scraping, clicking, dragging sounds. His shivers came from a place beyond the cold. Turning, he nudged Louise.

"Wake up, Louise. Wake up."

Louise yawned, stretched a bit, and opened the one eye nearest to Clark. "What is it?" she said sleepily.

"Listen. Something is coming." Clark's voice faltered. The scraping, dragging and clicking was louder than ever.

With a sudden realization, Louise jumped up. She wasn't safe in bed in the church basement. Staggering to her feet, she crept to the entrance of the hole. Clark followed. They poked their heads cautiously out into the open.

The shelf of rock was wet with spray, but there was no visible sign of anything else. But the sound was getting louder still. Whatever was making it was out of sight, around a bend in the rock shelf.

CLICK, CLICK. SCRAPE, SCRAPE. DRAG. CLICK.

With hearts beating faster, the two mice edged down the shelf. Louise got to the corner first and took a quick glance around the vertical face of rock. She let out a muffled squeak and threw herself backwards, almost knocking Clark down in the process.

"Run! Run! Run, Clark!" She pushed her brother back along the rock.

"What is it?" Clark's voice was high pitched with fear as he scrambled back along the shelf.

"Crabs. Large crabs. Crowds of crabs," gasped Louise. "Run. Don't talk. Run!" She slipped past Clark and ran along the ledge.

Clark looked back. Giant cruel pincers appeared, then the glistening eyes waving on stalks, the armored shell, the spindly spider-like legs, as the crab inched steadily towards the young mice.

Clark waited no more, scrambling and slipping on the wet rock of the narrow ledge after his sister. Below him the green ocean heaved up and down against the rock face. He willed himself to keep his eyes forward, fighting fear that was gripping his heart.

Louise let out a groan of despair and stopped suddenly. Clark collided with her and almost tumbled into the sea. The ledge came to an end just a few feet beyond where they now stood. A smooth, vertical face of rock loomed above them. The tossing waves of the sea burst into salty spray below them. Clark turned to look back. A line of crabs was now scuttling towards them, completely cutting off any escape. They were trapped.

Louise and Clark cowered up against the rock face, the salt spray blinding their eyes. The giant crabs scuttled steadily towards them, their clicking pincers waving menacingly before them. The young mice were paralyzed with fear. Then Louise screamed out, "Jump! Jump!" She leapt over the edge of the ledge and vanished into the foaming spray. Clark turned. A giant pincer snapped shut just inches from his head. He closed his eyes and jumped off the rock.

He struck the surface of the water. Suddenly, the sounds of the lashing waves were stilled as he sank into a foaming green tinged world. Then just as suddenly, he bobbed back up into daylight. He

Giant cruel pincers appeared, then the glistening eyes waving on stalks.

kicked out with all four feet to propel himself towards the rock. Its smooth slippery surface provided no handhold. His legs were getting heavy and he was starting to sink.

Then he heard a shout. It was Louise. He squinted through the salty spray. A piece of driftwood was bobbing up and down, and crouched on top of it was Louise.

Clark kicked out toward the driftwood and Louise hauled him aboard. The swirling current swept their makeshift

Clark kicked out toward the driftwood and Louise hauled him aboard.

craft out to the open waters. Clark looked back towards the rock shelf. It was now covered with crabs, their pincers waving to and fro in angry frustration. Any sense of relief was fleeting, as the towering waves of the unsheltered waters threatened to cast them into the deep.

The driftwood was tossed in all directions as the white-topped rollers thundered towards the shore. Blinded by the salt spray, the two mice clung to the wood as if it was part of them. Foaming white breakers surrounded them. There was a tremendous jolt; the driftwood had grounded. After a momentary lull, another wave swept them further ashore. The driftwood nose dived into the swirling water, struck hard, and catapulted its two riders into the air.

CHAPTER THIRTEEN

THE SANDCASTLE

Clark's landing knocked the breath from his lungs. He lay for some moments, his head spinning. He wiped the stinging seawater from his eyes. Louise was close by, gasping for breath but, like Clark, not seriously hurt. They had been thrown clear of the waves. The sand below was dry.

Louise groaned and climbed wearily to her feet. She sneezed, ejecting sand and seawater from her nose, and looked towards Clark.

"Some ride, eh?" she said, summoning up a cheeky smile.

Clark was in no mood for smiling. "We could have been killed." His voice shook with emotion.

Louise's confidence had quickly returned. "Don't be such a ninny Clark."

"Ninny?" snapped Clark. "We were almost flattened by motorbikes. We just missed being crab breakfast. And we nearly drowned. What does that tell you, cheese brain?"

Louise ignored the slight and her expression took on a superior look. "It tells me that we are on a roll."

"A roll!" Clark gasped in disbelief. "Progressively speaking. What should we do next? Jump off a cliff perhaps?"

Louise flashed a toothy smile. "Don't be silly Clark. It's just that the worst is behind us and we can head for home. And we still have the Pacific Ocean for Dad."

Clark looked at the small bottle still slung around his sister's neck. "Let's get going before all the tourists and their dogs come."

Without further discussion, Louise scampered off with Clark close behind. The dark outline of the dune stood out against the ever-brightening eastern sky. The blazing tip of the sun was already appearing above the horizon.

Clark's eyes watered as he squinted into the blinding light. He blinked away the tears and lowered his head, keeping his eyes fixed on the trail left in the sand by Louise.

A shadow flashed over the surface of the sand. He raised his head. Louise was still scampering on ahead, kicking back a spray of sand with every stride.

Another shadow crossed Clark's path. There was a rushing sound overhead. Clark's mouth went dry. He squinted into the sun. His watering eyes picked out dark shapes distorted against the shimmering light. Clark felt icy fingers clutching his insides. He instinctively swerved to one side. A fiercesome screeching pierced the air. Fear began to cramp his muscles. He staggered, almost lost his balance, but kept moving.

Gulls. The thought sent chills up his spine. He ran harder than ever. Where was Louise? More squawking sounds came from above. There was a rush of wings above him.

"Clark! Clark! This way. This way."

It was Louise. Clark followed the direction of the call.

It was coming from a large, abandoned sandcastle, which stretched out across the sand in front of him. In the gateway of its battlement walls stood Louise.

He collided with Louise and they tumbled, one on top of the other,
into the recesses of the castle.

Clark ran straight for the opening; he lost his balance just short of it, but his momentum carried him on. He collided with Louise and they tumbled, one on top of the other, into the recesses of the castle.

Fierce shrieks of frustration sounded from beyond the entrance gate. Then silence. A shiny black eye atop a cruel yellow beak appeared at the entrance to the castle.

They lay for some time as their heaving lungs recovered from the fearsome dash to safety.

Gradually, their eyes adjusted to the gloom and they were able to take in their surroundings. The castle walls were extremely thick and for that they were grateful. They could see light at the other end of the passage but decided to wait before exploring any further.

It was some considerable time before their jangling nerves had settled enough for them to set about investigating their situation. They crept towards the opening at the other end of the passage and cautiously poked their heads into the open, blinking in the bright light. They were in the central courtyard of the castle. It was square in shape and with two giant towers that reached up into the sky. They craned their necks as they searched for any sign of their winged attackers, but the blue canopy was only broken by fluffy white clouds.

Confidence somewhat restored, they studied the castle in more detail. It was well made and abounded in details. The interior square was paved with flat pebbles and the walls were decorated with shells of all shapes. In the middle of the pebbled square, a small round mirror had been placed to create the illusion of a water pool, reflecting the blue sky. A smooth ramp along one wall provided access to the battlements atop the stout walls. They slipped up the ramp keeping close to the wall. At the top they found a narrow walkway which ran all the way around the four walls. Further spiral ramps led up to the top of each tower. Louise, with a quick check of the sky above for gulls, climbed up one of the towers away from the sea. When she reached the top she carefully peeked through the battlements.

"What is it? What can you see Louise?" shouted Clark from below.

Louise did not respond immediately; she glanced down toward Clark. "You better come and have a look," she said quietly.

Clark climbed up the narrow spiral ramp, taking care not to look down. The higher he climbed, the more he became aware of sounds coming from outside the sandcastle. He heaved a sigh of relief when he reached the top. Louise was looking through the battlements. He took his place beside her.

Clark gasped out loud at the scene. The beach was no longer deserted. People were everywhere. People young and old, children large and small, dogs barking and running. And in the sky above them, jostling for space with the shrieking gulls, kites all shapes and colors of the rainbow, swooping too and fro, their tail ribbons trailing gracefully behind.

Louise and Clark could see the haven of the grass-covered dune beckoning from above and beyond the multitudes of beachgoers. "So near and yet so far," she sighed.

"What do we do now?" said Clark glumly.

"We will just have to wait until dark," said Louise. She looked up into the sky. "At least the crowds are keeping the gulls away from us. We are safe if we stay here."

"I'm not so sure," said Clark quietly.

Louise shook his head in exasperation. "Why do you say that? You are such a wet blanket, Clark."

"It's just that this castle is made of sand. And I remember that song the children sing at the church Sunday school," said Clark.

"What song?" asked Louise. She didn't attempt to hide the irritation in her voice.

"The one about the foolish man who built his house upon the sand and the rain came down and washed it all away. This castle is not only built on sand, it's also made of sand." Clark turned to look back towards the sea.

Louise gave out a loud sigh. "It's just a song. And anyway, it isn't raining, is it?"

Clark turned to his sister with worried eyes. "No. But the tide is coming in."

CHAPTER FOURTEEN

S.O.S.

Bert took a few deep breaths and started up the side of the dune. He had left Angus with Mavis and had made the excuse of going on a short stroll to get some fresh air. He had to get to the beach but if he should fail, he preferred not to be embarrassed by having someone with him.

Unbeknownst to anyone but himself, Bert had tried to go to the beach soon after he had recovered from the seagull attack. On his first attempt, the closer he had gotten to the beach, the tenser he had become. When he began to shake and have trouble breathing, he had been forced to give up.

He hadn't discussed it with Mavis or anybody else. After a few weeks he had tried again. But the second time had been worse than the first. The trembling feeling had started up and he had thought he was going to faint. He never tried again. As long as he kept away from the beach, he felt okay.

Now, as Bert limped up the dune, the shaky feelings started up. He was almost at the tall grass. He stopped and took a few more deep breaths. He was so close. He wished he had brought Angus with him, but it was too late. He thought of Louise and Clark, gritted his teeth, and carried on. His stomach churned over and over, but he was now pushing through the grass. The dull, distant roar of the surf was louder than ever. And suddenly there it was. The beach. He slumped down, breathing heavily.

The sun was high in the sky and the beach was a mass of activity. People were everywhere. Picnicking. Building sandcastles. Swimming in the sea. Flying kites. Walking. Running. Riding three wheeler bicycles. The area around the Haystack was particularly busy, as groups of people carrying cameras and binoculars studied the swarms of seabirds that soared and circled above.

Bert's heart sank. How could they have survived? And why had they done it? Tears started to fill his eyes. It was then he saw it. A flicker of light. The sun was reflected from something on the beach, close to the advancing surf.

"So here you are then? I thought you'd be here."

Bert turned quickly. It was Angus. The older mouse came and sat beside him. "We were getting a wee bit worried," he said quietly.

Bert sighed. "I'm sorry, Angus. It was a bit thoughtless, I suppose." He looked out to the crowded beach. "I just had to come here and ..." He didn't finish the sentence.

Angus nodded his head. "I understand, lad. Dinna vex yourself. I would have done the same if I was in your shoes."

Bert was not prepared to be comforted. "I should have spent more time with them, Angus. They wouldn't have wandered off if I had given them more attention."

"Few fathers spent as much time with their family as you have, Bert," said Angus kindly.

"But not lately, Angus," said Bert bitterly. "I spent so much time on the election. Being sick and all." His head slumped onto his chest.

Angus, at a loss for words, turned to look at the beach.

"Do you see that light flickering, down near the water's edge?"

Bert looked up. "Yes. I saw it. The sun reflecting off a piece of broken glass or something. It's coming from an abandoned sandcastle."

Angus was puzzled. "Funny. It seems to have a rhythm to it."

"It could be the wind," said Bert.

Angus shook his head. "Och, it's far too regular for that."

Bert suddenly became very interested. He stared towards the flickering light for some time.

"You're right Angus. Dot. dash. dot. dot. dash. dot. dash. dot."

Bert jumped to his feet. "It's Morse code, Angus. It has to be."

"What does it mean, laddie?" said Angus.

Bert was now very excited. "See the timing of the flashes, Angus. Short flash. Long flash. Then two more shorts. That is Morse code for L. Then long, short, long, short. That is C." He was now grinning from ear to ear. "Don't you see old friend? L and C. Louise and Clark. I taught them the Morse code last winter. It's them, Angus! It has to be them!"

Mavis and a group of neighbors came up upon Bert and Angus. "Have you found them?" Mavis asked anxiously.

Bert ran over and hugged her. "They're okay, Mavis. They're okay. They just signaled us. It's coming from inside that sandcastle."

Bert and Angus began to make arrangements for a rescue party to set off as soon as darkness fell. There was no shortage of volunteers. Angus suggested that they should all go home until nighttime. Soon he, Mavis, and Bert were left alone with just a few of Louise and Clark's schoolmates.

One of the younger mice climbed on top of a discarded soda can to get a better view. His keen eyesight confirmed that the flashing light was coming from the abandoned sandcastle.

Then the rhythm of the light changed. He called Bert's attention to it.

Bert carefully noted the new signal pattern. Dot, dot, dot. Dash, dash, dash. Dot, dot, dot.

"It is the international distress call, S.O.S. Something must be wrong." A cold flutter of fear entered his stomach.

"What can it be?" asked Angus.

Dot. dash. dot. dot. dash. dot. dash. dot.

Bert shook his head. "I've no idea, Angus." He licked his dry lips.

"It's the tide! The tide!" The young mouse on the soda can almost fell off with excitement.

Bert looked towards him. "What do you mean ..." his voice tapered off. A look of chilly understanding crossed his face.

He turned to look back at the beach. He tried to swallow the lump that had formed in his throat.

Mavis came along side him. "What's the matter, Bert?"

He turned his head slowly to look at his wife. "The tide, Mavis. It will wash away the sandcastle. The twins are trapped."

The flickering light continued on. Dot, dot, dot. Dash, dash, dash. Dot, dot, dot ...

CHAPTER FIFTEEN

THE BURGER BOX BOAT

It was clear to all that the choices available to Louise and Clark were limited and bleak. If they stayed in the sandcastle it would eventually be destroyed by the incoming tide. If they left the sandcastle they would be exposed to multiple dangers: humans, dogs, and the ever-present seabirds screeching and swooping in the sky above.

Bert maintained a grim silence for some time, the turned to his wife. "Why don't you head home and get some rest, Mavis? If anything changes, I'll send one of the youngsters to get you." He cleared his throat. "It will be some time before the tide reaches the castle and I'm sure they will leave it to the last moment before they make a break for it."

Mavis reluctantly agreed. She took the remaining young mice with her and headed for home.

As she passed out of sight, Angus cast a questioning look at Bert. "The tide is coming in very quickly Bert. It will be upon them very soon."

Bert nodded his head. "I know, Angus. I would rather she did not see what is going to happen next."

"And what would that be, lad?" said Angus.

Bert took a deep breath. "I'm going to go and bring them back, Angus."

Angus lost his normal composure. "Don't be so daft, Bert. This is no time for heroics. There is no way you can reach them, far less bring them all the way back."

Bert closed his eyes. "What else can I do Angus. If anything happens to them ..." His voice trailed off.

Angus gave out a loud sigh. "I understand, lad. Of course I understand. If I was younger, I would go with you."

Bert smiled. "I know that, Angus." He turned back to look at the beach. "What would be the best route to take, old friend?"

Angus shrugged. "There is no best, Bert. Maybe the least bad."

"What would that be?" said Bert.

"Well, the only route I can see that would provide any cover is the wee stream, down the beach there, that runs from the town out to sea."

Bert followed the direction of Angus's attention. Not far from where they stood a culvert pipe jutted out from the dune, and from it a steady cascade of water fed a small stream that meandered across the beach until it merged with the foaming surf. The rushing water carved its way into the sand, leaving a small vertical banking which would provide reasonable cover for a mouse.

But there where some obvious drawbacks. The stream was a favorite place of play for young children and their dogs. Even as they watched, a round, yellow tennis ball sailed through the air and splashed into the stream. A large, black dog sprinted across the sand, leapt into the stream, and splashed its way after the ball that was floating off towards the sea. Several small children joined the chase.

Bert exchanged a woeful look with Angus. "I see what you mean, Angus. Not very good odds." He watched the bobbing tennis ball as it coursed towards the surf. The speed of the current was sweeping the ball further and further away from the dogs and children.

"I wish I was that tennis ball. It has reached the ocean and look ... it's not far from the sand castle."

Angus turned to look at Bert. "Can you swim lad?"

Bert shook his head. "I'm afraid not. I always sink like a rock."

Angus pulled a piece of grass and started to thoughtfully chew the end.

Bert suddenly sat up. "Wait a minute though ..."

Angus raised his eyebrows, "What are you thinking, lad?"

Bert was now quite excited. "A boat, Angus! That's what I need. A boat!"

Angus looked more puzzled than ever. "Where will you find a boat, laddie? No mouse in the community has a boat."

Bert twitched his whiskers. "Where does that stream come from Angus?"

"It comes from a spring in the woods behind the town. It picks up some of the storm drains in the main street, runs through the public park, and then into the other end of the culvert."

Bert jumped to his feet and without a further word ran off through the tall grass.

He had already reached the small public park, which was on the other side of the dune, before Angus caught up with him.

He was standing on the grassy bank of the stream when a wheezing Angus came alongside.

"What ... are ... you ... up ... to?" Angus gasped out the words between breaths.

Bert laughed out loud. "Don't you see, old friend? I can set sail on this stream. Through the culvert and then on down the beach to the sea. The mouth of the stream is near the sandcastle. I pick up the kids and we drift down shore till we can find a quiet place to land."

Angus stared at him in disbelief. "Have you taken leave of your senses, lad? With a boat it would be a very long shot. And you don't have a boat."

Bert managed a brief smile. "That's where you are wrong, Angus. Follow me."

He ran over to a nearby deserted wooden picnic table. An overflowing garbage basket stood close by. Some paper bags and paper cups were scattered on the ground around the basket.

Bert scrambled around until he found a large yellow and red paper bag. He vanished inside and there were rustling sounds that ended in a squeak of triumph. He reappeared dragging along a polystyrene hamburger box.

He pulled it clear of the bag and turned to Angus. "What do you think, Angus?"

Angus looked more confused than ever. "Is this your boat, laddie?"

Bert nodded. "This is it, Angus. Polystyrene. Unsinkable."

Angus was speechless.

"Don't you see, Angus?" Bert continued somewhat breathlessly. "I can launch out from the stream bank here. Through the culvert and then on down through the beach."

"But somebody will see you." said Angus.

Bert shook his head vigorously. "No! No! I will keep the lid down until I reach the ocean. It will look like a piece of stray garbage."

"But when you reach the sea how will you steer ashore? You'll be at the mercy of the current. You don't have a paddle."

Bert vanished once more into the paper bag. After a few moments of muffled rustling sounds he reappeared holding a white, plastic coffee stirrer, which was almost as big as him.

"Here's my paddle Angus. And look. It even has an M on the end for mouse."

In spite of the seriousness of the situation Angus was unable to suppress a smile. In the presence of Bert's new born spirit he had acted like a wet blanket and he felt ashamed.

"Well, you better be on your way. Let's get the Queen Mary launched." They mice-handled the makeshift boat down to the water's edge. Angus suggested that they nibble a hole in the front of the lid to allow Bert to see where he was going.

Then Bert had another idea. He chewed out a hole at the rear of the box and stuck the paddle end of the stirrer through it to act as a rudder.

It was time to launch. Bert looked at his friend and gave a nervous smile. "I suppose I should get on my way."

Angus nodded, but looked troubled. "Why don't I go with you Bert? Two mice are better than one."

Bert shook his head. "No. I need you to stay behind, Angus. If anything should happen to me ..." Emotion tightened up his vocal chords. "I need you to be there for Mavis."

Angus nodded and put on a forced smile. "Okay, okay! You're not going to share the glory, so we better get you into the water."

They pushed the box down into the water. As Angus held on, Bert jumped aboard and grabbed hold of the makeshift rudder. Angus pushed the lid down shut.

"Okay, Angus. Shove off," came the muffled voice from inside the box. Angus gave the box a firm shove, sending it out into the stream and the swift moving current quickly drew the makeshift craft into the middle of the stream.

The speed picked up rapidly. Through the front port hole Bert could see the large dark circle of the culvert pipe entrance approaching rapidly. He leaned his weight on the stirrer as he tried to keep the box in the fast moving and deeper middle area of the stream.

The ride started to get bumpier as the culvert raced towards him. Suddenly he was in darkness and the amplified sound of the rushing waters was everywhere. Bert fought the fear that was gripping his heart. Then just as suddenly the box was out of the culvert. The sunlight diffused through the yellow lid of the box, casting a warm light inside.

The stream had become wider and shallower. The box struck an obstacle and Bert was thrown off balance for a moment. He almost lost the stirrer but just managed to grab the handle before it slipped out of the hole.

He leaned forward to get a better view out of the makeshift porthole. What he saw sent another chill running up his spine. A group of children were paddling in the stream up ahead. One was yelling and pointing towards the hamburger box. Another child crouched down and picked up a large pebble out of the water. The child took quick aim and threw. It struck just inches in front of the bobbing box. Water splashed through the porthole and soaked Bert. The box heeled over to one side. Bert shook the

The rock struck just inches in front of the bobbing box.

brine out of his eyes. The excited shouts of the children increased in volume. He took a cautious look out of the porthole just in time to see two other children launch pebbles.

The box rocked once more with a near miss. Bert held grimly onto the stirrer. There was a loud bang above him. The lid of the box was dented in and despair began to sweep over Bert. He wondered if it was only a matter of time before he'd be discovered.

CHAPTER SIXTEEN

THE RESCUE

Louise leaned the mirror against a battlement and slumped down beside Clark. "It's a waste of time. Nobody will have seen it."

"It was worth a try, Louise ... We had to try."

Louise took a couple of deep breaths. "I suppose so. But Dad is the only one who would understand Morse Code."

Clark stood up and looked down at the foaming surf. He swallowed hard. Each wave was closer than the one before. He watched the next one rolling ashore. It broke up into froth but kept on racing up the beach. Clark's cry of alarm was lost as the wave struck the front of the sandcastle. Seawater poured into the courtyard area and then was sucked back out by the retreating current.

Louise was already running down the ramp and Clark scampered after her. She vanished into the entrance tunnel and was digging up loose sand when Clark joined her at the front entrance.

"Dig, Clark! The castle will stand up longer if we stop the water coming in."

They dug away furiously, throwing the sand across the entrance. The next wave did not quite make it all the way to the castle walls and gave them enough breathing space to create a barrier of sand all the way across the entrance and half way up it. Another wave crashed into the walls and some water cascaded over their barrier, but it held. For the moment.

They retreated back up into the courtyard and wearily made their way up the ramp to one of the battlement towers farthest away from the approaching waves. They looked up and down the crowded beach. The incoming tide was forcing the people to retreat, resulting in an even more crowded situation between Louise and Clark and the refuge of the dune.

Gulls and multi-colored kites jostled for dominance of the sky. Dogs and children were running in every direction. Picnic groups seemed to occupy every open space.

"What do we do now?" said Clark, his voice pitched higher than usual.

Just then another wave raced up to the castle. A flood of seawater burst into the courtyard below... Their barrier had gone.

"We will have to make a run for it sooner or later," said Louise quietly.

Another wave struck. One of the towers shuddered under the shock. Diagonal cracks appeared in the side of the tower and it began to topple. Another wave thundered up the beach and the tower collapsed, taking part of the sidewall with it.

Meanwhile, another blow to the hamburger box sent Bert sprawling. The excited shouts of children were all around him. But the box kept moving. He still clung to the stirrer. A dog started to bark close by. The children's shouts began to indicate some alarm. The box had turned around and the porthole was facing back upstream. Bert got close to the hole and looked out. The children were scrambling out of the stream and a large black dog was splashing through the water in pursuit of the box, barking with every stride.

Bert started to paddle desperately to maneuver his craft back into the main current. The dog kept coming, but the water was getting deeper and the current stronger.

Bert managed to get the box going in the right direction and he lost sight of the dog. The barking continued but seemed to be less loud than before. Hope once more filled Bert's heart. The dog was falling behind.

He took a look ahead. The open sea was just a short distance away. He was now in the wide mouth of the stream. He pushed up against the box lid and it popped open; he stood up bracing his feet to counter the rocking box as it entered the rougher waters of the breaking surf.

There. Just a few yards away was the sandcastle, but his cry of joy was cut short as the front half of the castle toppled into the breaking surf.

"Dad! Dad!" The cry sent a thrill of relief through him.

He could now see Louise and Clark atop the remaining tower of the collapsed castle. They started to scramble down the remains of the ramp. Bert worked furiously with the stirrer to get nearer.

A wave caught the box and sent it skidding towards the crumbling castle.

"Jump! Jump, kids!" Bert dug the end of the stirrer into the sand at the bottom of the ramp to hold position. Louise and Clark scrambled over the sides of the box and collapsed on the floor.

The stirrer broke in half as the retreating tide sucked the box and the three passenger mice out to sea. The three clung to each other as their fragile craft was tossed to and fro by the surging waves. There was no time for greetings.

Bert took a look over the side. The current was carrying them down the beach, parallel to the shore and closer to the giant mass of the Haystack. The waves seemed stronger nearer the rock and were racing further up the beach. He looked back out to sea. A massive wave was coursing towards them.

"Hold on …" Bert just got the words out as the wave picked up the little box and swept it up the beach at breathtaking speed.

Foaming white water was all around them, spinning the box like a top.

Suddenly the box scraped to a halt. The waves were sweeping backwards out to sea. They were high and dry on top of a flat rock.

"The dune! Run for the dune!" cried Bert.

The three mice scrambled over the sides of the box and started run up the beach. People were all around. Shouting children and barking dogs came from every direction, but they kept their heads down and ran.

CHAPTER SEVENTEEN

THE KITE

There was a fluttering sound above them. Bert flinched as a dark shadow swept overhead, waiting for the expected and well-remembered cruel clamp of a gull's beak on his body. But it did not happen. He looked up as he ran. A large, white, diamond-shaped stunt kite was fluttering overhead.

A forest of legs and feet surrounded them. The three mice heard screams, shouts of glee, and barking dogs as they threaded their way through the crowd.

Then Bert heard the rhythmic thud behind him. He turned to look over his shoulder only to discover a large, brown dog in hot pursuit. Bert was breathing heavily. Louise and Clark ahead of him were beginning to stumble with exhaustion. The hot, labored breath of the dog was right behind him.

Suddenly the fluttering kite struck the sand ahead of them. The three mice tried to turn, but they tripped each other up instead, a jumble of fur, whiskers, and feet rolling on the ground just as the kite fell back on top of them.

The wet glistening nose of the dog sniffed around the edge of the kite.

"Hold on, guys." Bert grabbed hold of one of the plastic rods that made up the frame of the kite. Louise and Clark followed suit, holding on desperately as the dog tried to turn the kite over.

The snuffling nose poked under and raised one side of the kite. There was a sudden tug, a rush of air, and then the kite was streaking into the sky with the three mice clinging on for dear life.

Bert swallowed hard as he saw, for the second time in his life, the ground dropping quickly away below him. He managed to hook his rear legs over the rod to get a firmer hold. Louise and Clark had already done the same. They stared in fascinated fear at the ever-expanding view of the beach below them.

Suddenly the kite dove to one side. The air stream tore at the mice as the kite plummeted toward the earth. It leveled out a few feet above the sand, then zoomed once more up into the sky.

The wind stream vibrated the two thin control lines that connected to the unseen kite operator on the beach below. The kite took another horrific dive toward the ground and then swept back up into the sky. Up and up it soared into the heavens. Bert looked down. The people on the beach were looking smaller every second. There was a sudden jerk and the kite leveled out. It hung stationary in the sky, neither climbing nor falling.

In the brief bit of calm that followed, Bert noticed that the control lines were connected to the guy strings of the kite by two metal rings on each side of the center pole. An idea sprang into his mind.

"Pay attention, kids," Bert shouted above the wind stream. "I want you both to get close to those rings that the lines are connected to. One on each side of the center pole."

The two young mice inched their way into position along the cross pole. Bert's mouth was dry with fear as he followed their progress. He dragged himself along the center pole until he reached to where it was connected to the cross pole. The two young mice were now positioned on either side of him.

"Get your teeth around the lines and when I say NOW, bite through them. Quickly. At the same time. Understand?"

Both mice nodded and took hold of their lines in their teeth.

Bert looked down. The breaking surf was below them. The kite had leveled out for a moment.

"Now, kids! Now!" Bert shouted out.

Their timing was perfect; their sharp teeth sliced through both control lines at exactly the same moment. Instantly free of its ties to earth the kite jumped upwards. The vibrating of the lines and the drumming of the fabric faded into silence. The kite was motionless for a brief moment. Then the nose dropped like a rock, sending the kite into a steep dive.

Bert looked quickly left and right. The twins were still there, both hanging on desperately to the guy lines that had once connected the kite to the two control lines.

Bert worked his way back along the center rod. Gradually the nose began to lift. The horizon floated into view. The kite had leveled out. "How are we doing, guys?" He forced a hearty, confident tone.

"Okay, Dad," Louise responded shakily.

Bert turned to Clark, who was trying not to look down. "How about you, Clark?"

Clark took a deep breath. "What do we do now, Dad?" His voice quavered slightly.

"What we have here my dear children, is a kite which has become a hang glider. It just so happens I have studied the theory of flight, and if we keep her balanced and steady we will float back to the ground like a feather."

"But we are heading out to sea, Dad," said Louise. Bert looked ahead to the shimmering horizon where the sea merged with the golden tinged clouds.

"Yes, I see that, Louise. We have to do a turn and you both have to listen carefully to my instructions. I can adjust my position to keep control on the up and down, straight ahead stuff, but I will need your assistance for turns."

"What can we do, Dad?" Louise said quite sharply. "We are stuck out here on each side of you like a couple of hanging baskets."

"Exactly, Louise, but fortunately you both are about the same weight and this gives us balance." Bert forced another smile. "We will go left first so when I call out, I need you, Louise, to lean as far to the left as you can without falling off. When we have completed the turn I will shout to you to get back into your original position. Understand?"

Louise nodded her head. She was looking down at the shimmering blue of the sea far below, and to her left could see the giant mass of the Haystack Rock. They were almost level with its craggy top, a flurry of birds above it.

She turned to her father, "Shouldn't we go right, Dad, away from the Haystack?"

Bert shook his head, "No, Louise. There are up-currents of air flowing up the face of the rock that will lift us up to a higher altitude. We need that extra height if we are to glide beyond the beach, past the dunes to safety. We have no choice."

"But what about the seagulls?" Clark protested.

"Hopefully we will take them by surprise and be gone before they know what's happened."

The two young mice looked at their father, then at each other and exchanged looks of resignation.

Bert positioned himself at the intersection of the main longitudinal rod and the wing rod, the center point of the kite. "Okay, Louise, at the count of three." He eased his weight slightly to the left. The kite tilted in that direction. Bert took a deep breath. "One ... Two ... Three!"

Louise swung her weight to the left. The kite banked into a steeper turn as the air whistled through the guy lines. The massive bulk of the Haystack floated into view straight ahead.

Bert transferred his weight back on the central rod. The kite leveled out.

Louise let out a shrill cry. "The rock, Dad! We're going to crash! We're too low!"

"Stay still, Louise," Bert yelled out. "You too, Clark. Keep steady." He tried to swallow the lump in his throat. They had lost height in the turn. They were now below the summit of the Haystack and were heading straight for its steep seaward facing cliff. Louise froze and Clark closed his eyes.

Then suddenly a blast of cold air swept them upwards. The kite skimmed over the top of the Haystack and straight through a large throng of wheeling gulls who screeched out in fury as they scrambled to evade the speeding intruder.

Bert looked over his shoulder. The top of the giant rock was now behind and above them. The kite had already started to descend. Below his dangling feet he could see the waves surging towards the beach. There was no doubt, however, that the kite had gained some altitude. "What did I tell you? Up-currents of air. Just like it said in the book."

The pointed nose of the kite slammed into the unsuspecting bird.

Clark was squinting through watering eyes down towards the town. The houses seemed so small. Then he spotted a familiar shape. "Look, Dad! The Church! I can see the bell tower."

Bert nodded happily. "I can see it, Clark. We're almost home."

Louise meanwhile was studying the beach below. The holidaymakers dotting the beach looked like little bugs. She twisted her head around to look back at the Haystack Rock. Cold fear clutched at her heart. "Dad! Look! Behind us!"

Bert jerked his head round. A giant seagull was diving swiftly after them. It was gaining on them with every passing second.

"Hold on!" He screamed out. "We're going to dive." Even as he shouted the warning, he threw himself forward along the center rod. The kite plummeted downwards at an increasingly steep angle, the fabric of the kite vibrating against the rods as the air stream strove to tear it all apart. Bert glanced back. The gull was catching up fast.

He threw his weight forward to try to increase the angle of the dive. Bert's mind raced for a solution. Then he remembered another exhibition at the museum. *World War I Air War: 1914 to 1919*. He had been particularly interested in the air aces and their favorite air-to-air combat, dog fighting techniques.

Bert glanced back once more. The gull was closing in, its cruel beak already open in anticipation. They had one chance. "HOLD ON!" he yelled as he threw his weight back along the center rod. The kite swept upwards into a loop. Sand, sky, and clouds flashed before Bert's eyes. Sand reappeared below him. He thrust his weight forward again. Once more they were diving towards the beach. But now the gull was below them, looking from side to side, searching for the missing kite.

Bert let out a cry of triumph as the pointed nose of the kite slammed into the unsuspecting bird right between its shoulder blades. The kite stalled to a halt in mid air. The momentarily stunned seagull dropped like a brick out of view. Bert's shout of victory was cut short as the kite tumbled out of control earthwards.

"What do we do, Dad?" Louise yelled.

"Throw your weight forward," shouted Bert. "It's our only chance!"

Chapter Eighteen

Touchdown

Most of the Cannon Beach mouse communities were gathered on the lawn behind the church. The sun was dropping in the western sky and so were their hopes. Her neighbors surrounded Mavis, doing their best to comfort her.

Angus had just explained Bert's plan to reach the stranded children. "We have just had a report from some mice up at the dune that the sandcastle has now disappeared into the sea." He cleared his throat. "The broken up remains of a hamburger box washed up on the beach near Haystack." He glanced towards Mavis and blinked his eyes several times. "We all know that the young Clark was very keen on the church." There was some shuffling of feet amongst the listeners as Angus carried on. "So I think it would nice to join together in a spiritual song that expresses our desire for the safe return of our friends ... 'Amazing Grace.'"

Angus started off in full voice and one by one the onlookers joined in, including Mavis.

"'Amazing grace, how sweet the sound that saved a mouse like me. I once was lost, but now am found ...'"

As the song went on a dark object drifted across the bright sun.

"' 'twas grace that taught my heart to fear and grace my fears relieved ...'"

Angus squinted up at the object. A shout rose up from somewhere in the crowd. "Look! Look!"

The singing staggered to a halt as all eyes were lifted up.

"It's just a bird."

"No, no. It's one of those hang gliders."

"It can't be. It's too small."

"It's a kite, a kite. That's what it is."

"But there is no line. I can't see a line."

The kite banked over to one side and slipped closer to the ground. Then it began to make an 'S' turn directly overhead. The onlookers could now see three familiar shapes suspended underneath, a larger one in the front center and two smaller ones, one on each side.

It performed another slow turn over the church steeple and dropped closer to the ground. A faint voice sounded out from above the crowd. "Clear the way down there. We're coming in to land."

Mavis let out a shout of joy. "Bert! Bert! Angus, it's Bert!"

A ripple of excitement ran through the crowd, which quickly turned into shouts of disbelief, and then gave way to tumultuous cheers.

The white kite did a final pass overhead. They could hear Bert shouting instructions. "Lean left, kids. Good. Good. Straighten up now. Right ... lean right."

The craft did a graceful swooping turn. It was now descending quickly towards the ground. Bert could be seen adjusting his hold on the center rod to maintain balance.

The onlookers scattered in all directions. The kite skimmed low over the cabbage patch, its nose pitched upwards a fraction, and then it was over the soft, short grass. Bert's feet were the first to touch down. The kite pitched to one side. A wing tip scraped along the grass. The kite spun around, casting the three mice pell mell in the process, then skidded to a stop.

A crowd of would-be helpers ran towards the prostrate forms of the three mice. Mavis and Angus pushed through to the front of the crowd. "They're alive, Angus. Bert and the twins. Alive!" Mavis had to shout above the loud cheers of the crowd.

Angus slowed his gait, allowing Mavis to run on ahead. With tears in his eyes, he watched the joyful reunion of Mavis, Bert and the twins. "They are that, lass," he said reverently. "Very much alive and well."

———•••••———

Bert was elected headmaster of the Cannon Beach Mouse High School. Even his opponent voted for him. Hanging on the wall in the headmaster's office was a small bottle filled with gritty seawater. On a label were the words, "TO DAD. WITH LOVE. L & C."

As for the twins, the nicknames Loose and Clack were never heard again.

EPILOGUE

In a forgotten storeroom in the basement of the Smithsonian Institution in Washington, DC is the National Mouse Museum. In pride of place, suspended from the ceiling in the History of Mice Flight Section, is the Cannon Beach Kite with a plaque reading,

ON THIS KITE, THREE
RESIDENTS OF CANNON BEACH, OREGON
BECAME THE FIRST MICE
TO SUCCESSFULLY
COMPLETE CONTROLLED
FLIGHT.